JAY'S MAGIC BOMBER

By

SHEPHERD MOSS

PublishAmerica
Baltimore

© 2007 by Shepherd Moss.
All rights reserved. No part of this book may be reproduced, stored in a retrieval system or transmitted in any form or by any means without the prior written permission of the publishers, except by a reviewer who may quote brief passages in a review to be printed in a newspaper, magazine or journal.

First printing

At the specific preference of the author, PublishAmerica allowed this work to remain exactly as the author intended, verbatim, without editorial input.

All characters in this book are fictitious, and any resemblance to real persons, living or dead, is coincidental.

ISBN: 1-4241-8657-9
PUBLISHED BY PUBLISHAMERICA, LLLP
www.publishamerica.com
Baltimore

Printed in the United States of America

DEDICATED TO BETTY MOSS

My childhood sweetheart, wife of fifty-five years, greatest supporter, most truthful critic and best friend. She wouldn't let me quit.

ACKNOWLEDGMENT

Thank you to Julianne Papp
of
Brandon, Florida

Who gave direction and encouragement
to me in writing for young people.

INTRODUCTION

The year is 1944, and our country has been at war for three agonizing years. War is the topic at work, at school, at every family gathering, and at play. Children no longer play cowboys and Indians, but games of war. War news is a daily issue. You read about it in the newspapers, the monthly magazines, and the school's weekly reader.

Posters of military airplanes and ships are on display everywhere. They show American soldiers marching, sleeping, and eating in the rain and mud. Everything revolves around war and how each patriotic American, regardless of age, can help his country. Normal life is affected also. Drives in the country are no longer possible for a picnic or just to see the sights because gas and rubber are rationed. Items on the rationing list affect what we eat, what Americans wear, and how we play.

Caught up in this environment, an eager eleven-year-old paperboy with a vivid imagination stumbles across a large replica of a twin-engine bomber. The cockpit of this warplane looked big enough to allow a teenager to stand. Playing war will now have a real meaning. With this bomber, he would not need to use cardboard boxes and wooden crates for airplanes. He will no longer have to stand on the sidelines and watch others protect his country; he can help fight for freedom and justice for others. With his imagination and this war machine, his days will be transformed into patriotic dreams, heroic flights, and dangerous adventures.

Chapter 1
THE ADVENTURE BEGINS

The streetcar stopped a half block from the Strand Theatre, and eleven-year-old Jay jumped off and ran toward the long line that was sure to form in front of the theatre this warm Saturday morning in late August. Air-conditioned movie theatres were the only cool buildings in town in 1944, and on a hot day they were popular regardless of the movie. But today was special. Jay must be early because the doors opened at 10:00 o'clock, and the first fifty kids in line would receive an autographed picture of a movie star. Today's movie was "The Flying Tigers" with John Wayne. Jay must have that picture. Being tenth in line assured him a picture, but he would still have a thirty-minute wait before the line began to move.

Like everyone in line, he had five pounds of scrap metal in one hand and thirty-five cents in the other. He could buy a ticket, a bag of popcorn, a pack of Red Hots, and a coke.

The Army Air Corps advertised that they would be in the lobby exchanging the collected scrap metal for a pair of official Army Air Corps flier's goggles. Jay must have those goggles.

Finally inside the lobby, he looked around and saw the big cloud covered banner with airplanes printed on it. Across the banner were the words Army Air Corps. Posters advertising the Air Corps hung everywhere in the lobby. Jay knew the recruiting sergeant behind the table who handed out the flier's goggles in exchange for the scrap metal. When he stepped up to the table, the sergeant waved and spoke to him.

"Hi, Jay," he said in his friendly manner, "are you going to watch the picture twice today?"

"Only once, I guess," he replied, "I don't have enough money for drinks for the second show."

The sergeant motioned for Jay to lean over the table towards him.

"Listen, I'll buy the food and drinks for the second show if you'll come by the recruiting center to clean up a little," he offered. "Also, there's something I want to show you; I know you'll enjoy it," he whispered. He handed Jay the goggles, a brochure, and a quarter. Standing at attention, the sergeant gave Jay a military salute.

"Okay," he smiled and winked, "you'll do that, right?"

"Did you see that?" Jay heard the other kids around him talking, "That soldier gave him a real military salute."

Jay stood straight, pulling his shoulders back as he took the goggles and brochure from the sergeant and strutted away. He could feel the eyes of the crowd on him, and he felt proud.

Jay met the recruiting officer six months earlier when he stopped after school. He asked Jay to come in two or three times each week to sweep up the front office and empty the waste baskets into a large canvas bag called a burn bag. He went by about three o'clock in the afternoon during the summer months. He asked about the burn bag and learned that the soldiers took it to the back room where Jay could not go and saved it for a week. At the end of the week they took the bags to the city dump and burned everything in a deep hole, and then covered the hole with dirt. The back room was a mystery to Jay; they told him he couldn't go there for security reasons. As payment for his work, the soldiers gave him twenty-five cents and any military patches they might have. Once he got an air map of Europe.

Jay stopped at the candy counter for a bag of popcorn, Red Hots, and a coke, and then he rushed down front to get a good seat. He put on the flier's goggles to wear during the movie just like everyone else.

"Boy, do we look odd," he said to his neighbor sitting beside him. "Look, the light from the movie screen reflecting on our goggles makes us look like an army of flies," they laughed as the movie began to roll.

John Wayne, the hero, wore goggles just like the ones the recruiting soldier gave away. The action took place in China, where the United States was helping the Chinese fight the enemy. The American pilots flew real airplanes that were painted to look like tigers. The airplanes had eyes and a tiger's mouth with big teeth painted on the nose. Each pilot wore a flight jacket with two flags on its back, one of the United States and one of China, along with Chinese writing telling everyone that this man was a friend of China.

Jay's favorite movies were about war and airplanes. Every Saturday the Strand showed a war movie and sometimes a double feature with a western. All the military recruiters were there on some Saturdays. They each worked at a table handing out books on why you should join their group. A Red Cross nurse also worked asking for volunteers to help make weather clothes like hoods, gloves, and scarves for the soldiers. A girl sat at a table in the lobby selling war stamps and bonds. The government bonds helped to pay for guns, tanks, airplanes, ships, and all the equipment needed to fight and win the war. Posters in store windows, in school halls, on road-side signs and buses encouraged citizens to "Buy War Bonds and Stamps." Every movie carried frames at the end saying things like "America Needs Your Money — Buy War Bonds and Stamps At This Theatre." But Jay bought his stamps at school, so his school would be recognized in the district competition. They could win a patriotic banner for the most stamps and bonds sold.

Chapter 2
THE DETOUR

After the movie Jay usually went home through the city park so he could play airplane on the horizontal swings. There was a tall steel pole with a large metal "x" bar on top. At the ends of the "x" are long chains that hang down almost to the ground with a seat attached. If he could run fast enough or have someone pull him around, the "x" would rotate and cause the swings to go way out in space. It made Jay feel like he was flying. He loved to spend hours playing at the swings. But this Saturday he went home by the Library hoping to see some new pictures of Doolittle's air raid on Tokyo. He heard there were actual pictures taken from the inside of one of the B-25's on the raid. The B-25 was a medium range bomber that caught Jay's attention; he would have loved to go on that mission with Doolittle.

Next to the Library stood a small building that housed all the military recruiting offices: the Army, Army Air Corps, Navy, Coast Guard, and Marines. Each one had signs advertising why its branch was best. They were all patriotic with slogans like "WE WANT YOU," "JOIN THE NAVY AND SWEEP THE SEAS CLEAN," and "JOIN THE ARMY OR JOIN THE ARMY AIR CORPS." This is the building where Jay had his cleaning job in exchange for pamphlets, old posters and any old shoulder patches they might have. He sewed the patches of the air force on his leather flight jacket and the other services on a sweater. Both were covered with patches. Today, he went to the Army Air Corps office.

"Have you seen the pictures on the air raid over Tokyo?" he asked.

"Yes," the soldier replied, "it's interesting; you'll like it."

"Have you found any way I can help my country win the war?" Jay asked in a serious manner.

"You need to come back when you're seventeen," he answered, realizing Jay's concern.

Chapter 3
THE RECRUITER

Master Sergeant Raymond Wilson (Ray), the recruiter who handed out the goggles at the theatre, was a tall southern boy from Alabama with red hair and mustache and big shoulders. Above his nametag were several rows of campaign ribbons. Jay told him how much he liked airplanes and that he wanted to fly bombers like his uncle.

"What does your uncle fly?" he asked, looking down at Jay and smiling.

"He's the pilot in command of a B-26," Jay replied proudly. "He wanted to fly fighter planes, but he's too tall," Jay added.

"So he decided to try bombers?" Sergeant Ray inquired, showing interest in Jay's story.

"They sent him to Tampa, Florida, to teach him to fly the B-26." Jay continued.

"Did you know," Sergeant Ray said, "the pilots have nicknamed that bomber "The Widow Maker" because of the high number of trainee deaths. In fact," he continued, "they have a slogan: 'one a day in Tampa Bay.'"

Seeing Jay's interest in airplanes, Sergeant Wilson decided to share some of the recruiting information with him. He took Jay to a briefing room in that secret area and set up a movie about air corps training and lifestyle. Each airplane was described, and it explained how an airplane's control surfaces affected its movement. It explained why long-range high altitude bombers, medium and short-range bombers, attack bombers, night bombers, and fighters were needed. There were action pictures of daylight air-to-air fighters and air-to-ground support fighters. There were pictures of B-17's, B-24's, B-25's, B-26's (like his uncle flew), P-40's' P-38's, P-50's, P-51's, P-61 (Black Widow night fighter), and special variations of each. The B in front of the number stood for bomber and the P stood for pursuit, or fighter. It showed where the crew members were seated and described their duties.

The movie pictured models of airplanes in wind tunnels that showed all the moving parts of the wing and tail section and how the air traveled over the surfaces of the body, wings and all the controls. It explained the controls that help to move the airplane up, down, right, left, and through the air. There were flaps, a rudder, an elevator, a stabilizer, and the trim tabs. The flaps could slow the airplane down for landing or give it more lift on take off. Each part had a special job and could work with other parts to perform different functions. The part Jay liked best was when they showed the control panel and where the pilot sat. He knew that was the heart of the airplane. All the gauges, dials, and levers helped the pilot to control the airplane.

After the movie the lights came on, and Jay spotted the pilot's cockpit sitting in a corner of the room on a metal platform.

"That's a simulator," Sergeant Ray said, when he noticed Jay looking towards the platform. "The electric motors under the platform make the cockpit react like a real airplane," he said. "It's a training device that artificially duplicates the conditions and control of the aircraft under certain flight or combat operations. Do you want to sit in the pilot's seat?"

"Oh boy, do I!" Jay exclaimed, as he climbed into the simulator.

Jay noticed a panel with gauges. There were foot pedals, throttles, and a yoke with a wheel to guide the controls. He could push forward or pull it back to make the plane go up or down. Turn the wheel right, and the right wing dipped down; turn left, and the left wing dipped down. The wheel looked like half of a car's steering wheel. Sergeant Ray showed Jay how everything worked. Before he turned the motor on, he pointed to the instrument panel and told Jay what each gauge did. He pointed out the RPMs gauge with big numbers like 500, 1000, 1500, and 2000 showing how fast the motor turned. There was a bank and turn indicator, one for altitude, one that had a little airplane in the middle setting a straight line called the artificial horizon indicator, and many others that captivated Jay.

"All of this is important, of course; the instrument panel helps the pilot to fly," Sergeant Ray informed Jay, "but the most important factor is trust. The pilot's life depends on his trust and knowledge of his gauges." Finally he turned on the platform motors.

Needles on the gauges began to jump back and forth until they found their proper places. Pulling back on the wheel tilted the cockpit up; pushing it forward made it go down like a dive; turning the wheel right made the cockpit bank to the right; turning it left banked it to the left. The pedals on the floor made the plane turn right or left. The simulator had sounds of the engines like a real airplane. Sergeant Ray sat in the right (co-pilot) seat and explained each gauge and how it helped to fly.

"Jay, the most important gauge is the one with the little airplane in the middle," he explained. "See the horizontal line running through the middle of the gauge with the airplane on the line?" he asked. "If the little airplane's wings are even with the line, the airplane is flying level."

Jay flew several missions and made three landings during the next thirty minutes. He felt so excited to be learning about airplanes. Sergeant Ray Wilson, noticing the interest Jay had in flying, made the deal that day to extend Jay's cleaning for two more days each week at no extra pay, but in exchange for the use of the flight simulator when it is free.

"If you're interested, I can make you a junior flight cadet so you can fly in the simulator; only cadets and pilots are allowed to use this equipment," he said. "You'll have to keep your grades up and turn in all your homework too."

"Oh, I will," Jay replied excitedly.

"All right, Jay," the sergeant continued, "I'll have to swear you into the cadet corps," he said seriously, watching Jay's excited expression. "Do you swear an oath to keep any information you may hear or see in my office secret, and under the most excruciating torture you will remember that loyal patriots never break oaths or divulge secrets."

"Oh yes, I swear," Jay responded, as he raised his hand to signal an oath.

Chapter 4
THE ENLIGHTENMENT

After turning off the platform motors, Sergeant Wilson took Jay to his desk and gave him some recruiting pamphlets.

"What does a person have to do to be an Army Air Corps pilot?" Jay asked, as he leafed through the pamphlets.

"Here I'll show you the test we give to everyone who wants to be a pilot," he said, passing the paper for Jay to see.

"Gee whiz," Jay exclaimed, "There are words I've never heard of or could even pronounce!" He continued, "This math part is really something else; they use numbers and letters in their problems."

"Yes, you have to know those equations to qualify for flying," Sergeant Ray explained.

"It looks more like a special code than math problems," Jay replied, "This must be a very new advanced type of math. Why do you have to use math to fly an airplane?" Jay questioned.

"The kind of math pilots use is what I call "walk around arithmetic," he replied. "It's flight math," he continued explaining. "Flying is more than sitting in a cockpit guiding an airplane through the air; you use math in calculating weights and balances. A bomber has to have fuel, bombs, and men. All these things add weight." He watched Jay's eyes get bigger, "From the time the engines start until the mission is over, the pilot or navigator has to use math."

Sergeant Ray put his arm around Jay's shoulder and led him over to a big map on the wall. "Do you know where England is on this map?" he asked, smiling.

"Yes," Jay said, pointing to some islands off the west coast of Europe.

"Correct," he replied. "Now, let's say you're going to make a bombing run from England to Germany, okay?" He pointed to the map to show the area. "We don't want the Germans to know our target for tonight, so we use evasive action. Are you with me?" he asked.

"No sir, what is evasive action?" Jay asked.

"Well, let me see," he looked up toward the ceiling for a moment. "Okay," he continued, "when we take off from England and fly over the channel, the Germans know we're coming because of their aircraft spotters. Do you know what a spotter is?"

"Yes, aren't they people who watch for airplanes in the air?" he responded, proud he knew the answer.

"Okay, they are placed up and down the French coastline," he explained, "When they hear our planes, they report to their headquarters what kind of planes, how many, what altitude we are flying, and the direction we are moving. With this information, they try eagerly to guess which city is going to be bombed. Are you with me now?"

"Yes sir," Jay answered, "but how can they do that?"

"Good question, son," he replied smiling.

"Let's say there are one hundred B-17's flying at 25,000 feet heading due east. The B-17 is a long-range bomber, so that means the raid will be deep inside the country. The number gives them some idea of the target—one hundred B-17's carry tons of destruction and can fly deep into France or Germany, complete the mission, and return to home airfields," Sergeant Ray watched Jay's expression to see if he was listening.

"The type of escorts tells them something too," he continued. "If the escorts are P-51's, that means it's more likely to be a deep raid inside of France. The direction will help them pick one or more target cities, so they can alert their air force and warn them of a possible raid. Are you with me now, son?" he asked again.

"Yes sir, I think so," he replied.

"Good," he continued, "now after take off, we fly east for three hours. That's about three hundred miles. At this point half of our group turns northeast. Now we have two groups of fifty planes each flying into enemy territory. This makes the Germans think there might be two different targets. We'll meet the other group later over the French and German border. Our group is still heading east. Also half of the escorts went with the break away group. After thirty minutes on this course, we'll turn north to Germany," he pointed his long stick at the map.

"Here, let's do it this way," he said, taking some string and thumb tacks. He pointed to the map and tacked one string over the word London in England, stretched the string over to Paris, France, and placed another tack. Stretching the string north to Germany, he stopped at Berlin and placed another tack.

"When we get to Paris, we turn north and head to Germany. By this time the Germans know we are coming, but they don't know where we plan to bomb," he continued talking while he placed his finger on the border of France and Germany. "During the four hours of flight, we have used half of our fuel. All of the flight the navigator uses flying math to calculate our position. Using the weight of the plane, its load, the head winds, and flying speed, he checks to make sure we are on course and will be over the target on time," he paused and continued, "and also one more important item." Pointing to the map he said, "Remember the group that left us back here? Their navigator is working just as hard as ours."

"You see, all of us have to meet right here at the same time," he said, again pointing to the map. "This is not an easy task—we're flying at night. Remember while we're flying, we use fuel, that means less weight in the airplane. By the time we get to the target, we'll need to have enough fuel for our alternate target in case of bad weather and, of course, the return home. All these calculations are done by using what you called new math," he paused and thought for a moment, "This is why you need to study hard, make good grades and come back in six or seven years." He smiled and patted Jay on the back.

"Yes sir, I see, but I have another question," Jay replied, "Why couldn't we fly from our country over the North Pole and slip in behind all these airplane spotters?"

"That's a good theory, but that would require a new type of silent engine, very fast and uses less fuel," Sergeant Ray conceded. "We don't have anything like that right now. Maybe by the next war, or when you learn to fly, but not now." They walked over to his desk.

"I have to close now, but maybe you can use these?" he handed Jay an old set of air corps wings, an Eighth Air Corps patch and some old air charts of Europe. "Look, son, you're doing a very important job by collecting tin and scrap iron for the war effort. Young soldiers like you collect half of the metal used in airplanes and tanks. Keep up the good work," Sergeant Ray exclaimed.

"Thank you for spending time with me, letting me ride in the simulator, and for the patch and charts," Jay said graciously. The sergeant saluted Jay again.

"I can't believe I've been saluted and called a young soldier all in the same day," Jay thought, as he left the recruiting office.

Chapter 5
BIG BILLY THE BULLY

Leaving the recruiting office, Jay walked next door to the Library to see the new pictures of the Doolittle Raid. As he started up the steps, he heard someone crying in the bushes on the other side. Curious about the crying, he went to see what happened. Roger, a friend from school, lay on the ground pinned down by Big Billy, the school bully. He sat on Roger's stomach facing his feet and emptying Roger's pockets on the ground looking for money. That's how Billy got his spending money. You gave it to him when he asked, or he would take it from you. Billy's three back-up boys were in a circle at Roger's head standing on his hands. Roger couldn't move. The boys didn't hear or see Jay approaching from behind.

"Hey, fatso, get off Roger," he blurted out without thinking. He surprised Billy as well as himself. Billy turned to see who spoke. Billy's mouth and eyes scrunched up in his famous "scare you to death" look when he saw Jay.

"He's thinking about the run-ins we've had before," Jay thought, as he waited to see what Billy's next move would be. "I held my own when he was by himself, but when his goons are with him," Jay reasoned. "I can outrun Billy, but not all three of his goons."

Billy got up off of Roger and started for Jay with his friends close behind. Roger slowly got to his feet. His legs looked wobbly as he started picking up his things off the ground. He took a couple of uncertain steps backwards, turned, and started running for the Library doors.

"I sure hope he's going for help," Roger thought, as he waited for Billy to make his next move.

"That's it four eyes, run and hide under a table," Billy yelled after Roger.

Jay was on his own. Alone. Billy and his thugs walked slowly toward him. The expression on Billy's face told Jay that he was in trouble, probably going to get beat up a little.

"Well, well, well, if it isn't the class dreamer," Billy said, as he and his bully buddies came toward Jay.

"I must keep on talking so I won't have time to get scared," Jay thought, as he tried to hide his fear. "If I talk big and tough, he might leave me alone," Jay reasoned to himself, as he stood his ground. "I must not back up so he won't know how scared I am."

"What's an over stuffed Frankenstein and his three stooges doing hanging around the Library?" he asked, bravely looking into Billy's eyes. "You have to know how to read before they'll let you in there, Pilgrim," he plodded on trying to sound like John Wayne.

He remembered that when Billy was angry, he became annoyed. And when he was annoyed, he was easier to manage. Billy didn't expect anyone to stand up to him.

"And," Jay thought, "if Roger doesn't hurry back with help, I may not be standing very long." At their last meeting, Jay caught Billy by surprise. He didn't expect that would happen again.

"Now he will try to even the score," Jay thought. "I have to think fast or I'm a dead duck."

"How's the nose, Billy?" Jay managed to ask without his voice shaking. "Call off your three goons and I'll make it two out of two."

Billy confronted Jay before when they were both alone. Jay felt he was lucky that day. Billy backed him against a wall and was about to turn him into a red spot on the cement. Jay remembered what his uncle taught him. He could hear his uncle's voice in his head: "If you can't talk your way out of a bad situation, strike the first blow and make it count," Jay remembered. "Step into an oncoming punch and land the hardest blow you can right to the side of the other person's nose," Uncle Ralph continued. "Nothing hurts worse than a hard nose strike. When you step into his punch, you just might throw him off balance, and a person can't throw punches when he's off balance."

Jay used his uncle's advice and it worked. Billy's hand just glanced off Jay's left shoulder, and he started falling forward. As he fell, Jay landed a blow to the left side of his face hitting his nose with a fierce blow. Billy's head turned with the force and his eyes were wide in bewilderment. Jay moved quickly to get out of his way. "If Billy fell on me, I'd be flatter than a dime," Jay thought.

When Billy fell beside him, Jay noticed blood gushing from his nose like water from a faucet. While still lying on the ground, Billy grabbed his nose with both hands and let out a howl that sounded like a herd of buffalo. He didn't look so big and mean lying on the ground with blood all over his face and hands. Jay stumbled toward him, not to hit him again, but to help him up. Even though the blood wasn't Jay's, he felt scared. He just knew he broke Billy's nose. Just then, Jay thought, "If I help him up, it might be a sign of weakness that will cause Billy to think I'm afraid of him — maybe now he'll leave me alone."

"Don't hit me again, Jay," Billy raised his bloody left hand and cried.

Holding his nose with his right hand, he slowly got to his feet.

"He thinks I'm coming after him for the kill," Jay chuckled under his breath. Billy's eyes were as big as dinner plates, and he looked around to see if anyone witnessed his defeat. No one was in sight so he cut and ran.

Jay asked Billy about his nose because he knew Billy didn't tell anyone about the previous fight, especially his buddies. Jay didn't tell anyone either; it was between Jay and Billy. He felt sure Billy remembered that day and now could get even.

Billy stopped his advance and motioned for his three buddies to stay back. They stood looking at each other for a moment.

"I hope Mother recognizes me when they carry me home," Jay thought, "I can hear it now."

"Mrs. Young," the policeman would say, "this is the way we found him at the foot of the Library steps. He must have fallen down all those steps and then a park truck ran over him. But don't worry, he's still breathing."

Jay stood his ground, brought his hands up to his waist, turned his shoulders a little bit and made a fist. Turning his shoulders allowed him to step out of the way when Billy charged, at least, that's the way they did it in the movies. Billy stooped down in his famous "charging bull" stance, pawed the ground with his feet and started to take a step, then stopped. The mean look on his face would "curdle milk" as Jay's mother would say. Billy stopped his show of the charging bull, straightened up, almost smiled and waved his hand in a salute.

"Get you later, Jay," he said, as he turned and ran with his three buddies right behind him.

"What's that all about?" Jay thought, as he relaxed a little. Then from behind he heard Sergeant Ray's voice.

"You better join the Marines if this is a sample of your day," he said, placing his hands on his hips. "I saw what happened; you need to check on your friend, son. I like what you did; I'd have you on my crew any day," he added. He saluted Jay and walked away.

Jay started up the Library steps when he saw Roger coming out the doors with Miss Whitford, the Librarian, and the janitor right behind him. Miss Whitford wanted to know if Jay was all right, and she wanted the names of the boys that started the fight.

"I'm okay," he said, "I don't know their names. I've seen them hanging around the Library shaking down kids for their money."

Jay pointed across the street and told her that he and Roger lived three blocks over that way. He said he would take Roger home for his mother to care for him. He wrote his and Roger's names on one of the Army pamphlets and gave it to Miss Whitford. She said she needed them for her report. She asked again for the names of those ruffians. Roger started to answer, but Jay winked and shook his head no. Roger got the message and didn't say anything.

25

"Are you sure you're not hurt?" Miss Whitford asked again. "Is everything all right?"

"No ma'am, we aren't hurt," Jay conceded, "and as far as I know, everything is okay."

She went back in the Library and Roger and Jay went on their way. Jay didn't get to see the Doolittle pictures after all.

Roger was disturbed that Jay didn't tell the Librarian about Billy and his stooges.

"Look, Roger," Jay explained, "the best way to keep Billy off your back is to keep him guessing. I'm sure he saw Miss Whitford talking to us. They were over in the park watching from one of the baseball field dugouts. He saw me give her the pamphlet and point to his house. He doesn't know what was on the paper, or what I told her when I pointed." Jay continued explaining, "For all he knows that paper had his name on it, and I pointed to where he lives. Later I will tell one of his bully buddies that they are being watched. He will think twice before bothering you again. I think he's expecting something to happen soon. And when it doesn't, he won't know what to think. He's always in trouble so maybe that will hold him for awhile."

"Okay, Jay," Roger agreed. "Thanks for helping me," he said, as he left to go home.

On the way home Jay stopped by Mr. Brown's house, the district manager for the newspaper, to pick up some release forms for his mother to sign. Jay wanted to deliver papers, and Mr. Brown had a job opening for a paperboy. But Jay wasn't sixteen so a parent had to sign for him.

"Everything I want to do, I'm told, 'you're too young, son,'" Jay exclaimed. "Life is hard to understand at times. We're always being told, 'you're too young for this or that,' and in the next breath we're told 'you're old enough to know better.'"

Chapter 6
THE SUMMER DAZE

Eleven-year-old Jay, who stood a head taller than most other boys his age, believed he was old enough to be a paperboy. If he worked at it, he could pass for thirteen. There were only four qualifications a person needed to be a paper boy: strong enough to carry a bag full of folded newspapers, tall enough so the full bag doesn't drag the ground, a good strong throwing arm, and brave enough to face the dark and dogs.

Jay reasoned that he knew how to read, could follow directions, and could read a map so why couldn't he have the job. It would give him spending money and let him be patriotic and help in the war effort. He could pick up empty bottles, scrap metal, and old newspapers. He could still be a useful soldier—maybe he isn't old enough to fly an airplane, but he can help build those planes.

That evening Jay cleaned the dinner table and helped his sister wash dishes—to please his mother and put her in a good mood.

"Mother, I'm eleven years old and big enough to throw newspapers," he said, feeling confident.

"No," she said emphatically, "you may be eleven, taller than your friends, and willing to work hard, but that doesn't make you a man," she added. "It takes a man to get up that early and go out by himself in the dark to work."

"Oh, come on, Mom," Jay argued. "You're always telling me that since Dad is away so much, I'm the man of the house. If I'm old enough to be the man of the house, I'm surely old enough to throw a few papers in the dark."

"No, it's dangerous out there in the dark by yourself," she repeated.

"Ah, Mom," Jay snapped back. "In Hungary boys my age are carrying guns and shooting Germans and they are shooting back," he continued begging. "If they can do that, why can't I throw a few papers in a city that's not in a war zone? I don't need to worry about someone throwing them back," he smiled sheepishly.

"James Albert Young," she demanded, "what part of 'NO' do you not understand?" When she used all three of his names, he knew things weren't going his way.

"Mother, please," Jay pleaded, "When I play war, you tell me I'm too old for that sort of stuff, and I should start acting like a man. And when I want to act like a man and help with the war effort, you tell me I'm too young," he whined. "How old should I be to stop acting like a boy and start being a man? Other boys in my class work…"

"That's enough," she interrupted, "You never know when to stop; you are just like your Dad. You walk and talk like him, and you even have the same hairline," she observed. "You made your point; now finish your chores."

"I have," Jay exclaimed, "and I've finished my homework too," he added.

"Go on, get out of here," she scolded. "Play with your brother, and I'll think about it—just think, mind you."

"Bet the part about being the man of the house helped me," Jay thought as he went to find his baby brother.

Jay really felt like the man of the house when his Dad was out of town for two or three months working his special trade at war plants in different cities. He tried to come home on weekends, but because of gasoline rationing, travel was limited. At first he tried to take his family with him, but that didn't work out. Finding a place to live with children was almost impossible. When he did find a place, it was a real dump. One place out west was a really old shack. The kitchen had a hand pump for water, and the sewer emptied into a ditch behind the house. His Dad wouldn't let them drink the water or use the pump at all. He put a bucket over the pump and nailed the handle to the counter top. They got their water from their next door neighbor after his Dad made a 'real deal' with him. In exchange for drawing water from the neighbor's well and then using his goat cart to transport the water home, they milked his three goats every morning — he did the milking at night — and Jay's Dad also gave him some of his extra gas ration stamps. Because of his job code, he was given more stamps than other people. Jay's Dad tried to enlist in the military, but his trade was considered even more important to the war effort than the Army.

Jay had a brother and a sister, and his mother was now expecting another baby.

"If you don't mind me and do as I ask, I'll give you another sister," she threatened.

"Well, I try to do everything she wants, and sometimes more, because I don't want another sister; one in a man's lifetime is enough," Jay reasoned.

He waited a few days before asking his mother about the paper route again. By that time she had heard what happened at the Library. Roger's mother told her how he saved her boy from certain death at the hands of a big bully.

"Mother, what about the paper route?" Jay asked, being careful to add that it would teach him responsibility and how to manage money.

"Well, okay," she relented, "but you be careful."

"That's how mothers are when they agree with you," Jay thought. "They have to add a little advice to show they are still the boss."

The next day Jay went to Mr. Brown's house to pick up his paper bags, the route ring, a paper punch, and a map of his customers. The bag was a large canvas bag with a strap to go over his head and rest on his shoulders. He had two of these bags with the name of the newspaper on each side. His route ring was a large brass ring that held cards with his customer's names and addresses. He used it to collect his money each week from his customer. He had to keep records by punching a hole in the card.

After a week of throwing the papers, Jay discovered the job was more difficult than he thought. He got up every morning in the darkness, went to his pick-up station, and folded ninety-five papers, placing them neatly in the two bags. Gathering his bags, his customer card ring, a map, a flashlight, and a stick to scare dogs away, he was ready to throw newspapers. At first he thought three hands were needed to throw papers.

The first day he spent more time picking up things he dropped than delivering the route. By the fifth day Jay managed a balancing act that allowed him to throw the route with ease. The dogs began to know him and followed him every morning. Maybe it was because he carried treats with him to appease them, that he felt safe enough without the stick. Soon he learned the route and could leave his ring and map. But he needed the flashlight because in the dark he struggled with one big problem — his imagination.

"Your imagination is as big as the State of Texas, and it's going to run away with you someday," Jay's mother often said.

"Boy, at times, did it ever," Jay thought, as he tried to whistle a happy tune, but his lips were so dry he couldn't make a sound. The light helped to change his imagination into reality.

Chapter 7
THE WITCHES AND MONSTERS

Jay didn't have a bicycle so he walked the eight blocks to the paper drop station each morning. Because of the war shortage, he didn't have rubber bands to hold the papers. They must be rolled a special way so they could be thrown without coming apart. Throwing the paper wasn't so hard, but it sure was dark. Streetlights were shaded because of the war, and early morning darkness seemed creepy and quiet. Jay missed the normal daytime noises such as cars, trucks, buses, or streetcars. Every little sound seemed amplified many times louder. Houses, trees, bushes, and poles took on different shapes. The first morning Jay thought he heard a witch flying above the trees. He fell to the ground quickly and tried to shine the flashlight up in the trees to see her. But he broke the light when he fell. Imagination caused him to miss throwing ten customers the first day.

The next morning, halfway through the route, a storm moved into the area. The wind in the pine branches and needles made a rustling sound and the breaking of branches snapping and hitting the ground frightened him. The wind blowing the limbs back and forth and the singing of the pine needles along with the blackness reminded Jay of the movie, "Frankenstein Meets Wolf Man." At times falling branches became tangled in electric power lines and made sparks like the fourth of July—sounded like Rice Krispies, "Snap, Crackle & Pop."

By the third morning, Jay determined that he would ignore the breaking branches, whistling wind, and the dogs sneaking up behind him with their cold wet noses against his hand. The more he tried to avoid thinking about being scared, the more he noticed the trees and weird shapes around him. Fast growing Kudzu, a large-leaf ivy, covered the bushes and hedges causing them to look like monsters, long lizards, and other frightening shapes. His mother was right; he had to control his imagination.

Having survived the first week, Jay felt stronger and more relaxed rolling and throwing the papers. He started reading the headlines and looked for pictures and stories about the Army Air Corps.

Everyday in Miss Clements's class, they were asked to read and discuss the headlines in the newspaper. Jay always had a good report. He read the paper as he folded it. This morning the big story described an unsuccessful raid on an oil refinery and ball bearing plant deep inside Germany.

Chapter 8
THE BOMB RUN

Jay's paper delivery took just over an hour to complete. The time passed quickly as he made a game of throwing the papers. He managed to control his fears of the darkness and the monsters and witches. He could only imagine one scene at a time, so he concentrated on playing a war game with his papers.

He pretended to be an airplane and his rolled papers were bombs. Every front porch made a target. He threw the papers to make direct hits with his pretend bombs—never a miss. How could there be anything else? When he wore his leather jacket with the gold pilot wings on the front over the pocket and the military patches on the sleeves, he couldn't miss.

Chapter 9
THE BROWN BOMBER

Jay always looked for ways to improve the paper route and make the work easier, more fun, and still make money. One morning he decided to cut through Roger's back yard to the next street. He had not been in Roger's back yard, so he didn't know if the way was clear. But if he could find a short way between the two streets, it could save him five minutes on his route. He could avoid going all the way around the next block.

As he rounded the corner of Roger's house, something caught his eye in the moonlight. He stopped so fast that his bag flew by him and pulled him to the ground so that he fell on his knees. Something big stood back under the trees.

It looked like an airplane. Not in Roger's back yard; he didn't like airplanes. He wouldn't play games about airplanes or go to a movie about airplanes. Nevertheless, there was something big standing under the trees. The moonlight filtering through touched on a wing and an engine. A big airplane! HOLY SMOKE!! He couldn't believe his eyes.

In the corner of Roger's back yard in the shadow of the big oak trees stood a brown, twin-engine bomber. A B-25! As Jay moved closer he could see all the markings of a real Army Air Corps bomber. It wasn't as big as a real one, but it looked big enough to get inside. It looked longer than his Daddy's car. Much longer.

Chapter 10
THE DREAM IS REAL

Jay walked around the beautiful airplane two or three times touching the fuselage, looking in all the windows, turning the propellers, moving the flaps and all the controls. Gee Whiz! It even had wooden guns for all the turrets. Everything was so realistic—it was swell! Jay could not believe this treasure stood in Roger's back yard all this time, and he had never said anything about it. He had known Roger three years, and Roger had not talked about his parents or the airplane. In fact, Roger didn't mention anything about the war or wanting to play war. All he talked about was schoolwork and special projects. He would go with Jay to collect scrap metal, and he would hang out at Jay's house. But Jay knew Roger was sweet on his sister.

"It could pass for one of Jimmy Doolittle's B-25's that bombed Tokyo," he thought, as he continued to admire the airplane. He looked for a way inside. Then, he remembered his paper route.

"I'd better finish throwing papers, and then if I have time, I'll come back to investigate the bomber," Jay told himself, as he thought about how many more customers he must throw. He ran all the way throwing the last twenty customers very quickly.

He returned to Roger's yard fifteen minutes later and spent about thirty minutes before the sun came up.

"Holy Cow!" he whispered. "I can't believe this is happening." He touched the bomber again to make sure it was real.

Only the pilot's compartment, top gun turret and tail gunner's compartment had glass—well, it wasn't really glass, but maybe something like Plexiglas. The cockpit window where the pilot sits was higher than the others, so Jay stood on his toes to see inside. Through the darkness he could make out two seats with all the control panels and dials like a real airplane.

He let the empty paper bags slide slowly off his shoulders, and falling down to the ground, he crawled under the bomber looking for a way to get inside. Feeling his way along in the grass, he touched something furry and warm with his right hand. Jerking his hand back, Jay could feel the thing roll up and curl toward him. Falling backward, he landed on his hands and feet with his stomach upward.

"I must look like some kind of weird insect," he said to himself.

Rolling to one side and jumping up to get out of the way, he struck his head on the bottom of the fuselage. Then he fell back on the furry thing again. He started rolling back under the wing until he touched another round furry thing. This one stood on its tail until its nose reached the bottom side of the wing—almost four feet from the ground. Trying to get away again, he found himself in the same position as before, on his hands and feet with his stomach in the air. He could move backwards faster than he could run. When he finally found himself in a standing position, he hurried back to his paper bag to get his flashlight. Very cautiously, he went back to the wing and found that furry thing.

As his flashlight beam slowly moved along the ground, he spotted the round furry thing that had him so scared. There it was; a frayed rope, securing the airplane to the ground. He found more rope on the other wing and on the nose wheel. Jay didn't know why, but he looked around to see if anyone noticed his ridiculous behavior. He really must get a grip on his wild imagination.

Once more he crawled under the bomber. This time he took his trusty flashlight looking for a way inside. For a change, he thought, luck was with him, and he found the bomb bay doors opened. Crawling inside he noticed a bizarre feeling came over him as he looked around. He felt like a real Army Air Corps pilot and this plane looked like a real bomber—a bomber that could fly dangerous secret missions from Roger's back yard.

Chapter 11
THE PREPARATION

Once inside the bomber, he had to wait for his eyes to adjust to the darkness. He feared using the flashlight because of being discovered and the police called. He didn't think Roger's mother would mind him being in the bomber. But in the darkness she might not recognize Jay. Daylight should be near.

Moving forward to the flight deck, he could see wires running overhead from the cockpit to the tail—control wires for the rudder, elevator, stabilizer, and trim tabs. Just like those shown in the recruiting movie.

Once in the pilot's seat, he could see that everything looked just like it did at the recruiter's office in the simulator. It looked like a real cockpit even down to the dials, clocks and the pedals on the floor.

Looking out the window at the engines made him feel as though he sat in a real cockpit. He could feel the plane shake as the engines tried to start. He yelled out the window, "Clear on number one and two." The propellers started to turn, smoke poured out the exhaust pipes, flames shot out from under the cowling vents, and he could hear the engines running and the wind and clouds rushing pass the windows. Holding his hand to his mouth as though he had a mike, he tried to contact the tower for landing instructions.

"Tower, this is Bomber B-25 requesting active runway, wind direction and other information needed to land this thing," he said, trying to be quieter. "Wow, this is going to be fun. Wonder if this bomber could help in the war effort," he thought, as he continued to investigate the gauges.

Jay sat there a long time dreaming of high adventure and dangerous missions, and the one thing he knew for sure.

"Those monster trees, bushes and hedges will not be on my mind again," he declared.

Looking around he could see dead leaves, pine needles, and some small branches that must have come in through the open side gun station windows. The inside must be cleaned out.

While cleaning the debris out of the cockpit, he discovered a drawer under the pilot's seat. Opening it he found diagrams, detailed sketches, instructions, and blueprints for building the bomber. A brown envelope with Roger's name slipped out of the drawer. Inside was a letter addressed to Roger. When Jay opened it another letter fell out. The letter was from Roger's Dad.

"To my beloved son," it started out. Jay closed the letter back and put it inside the brown envelope without reading it. The other piece of paper looked more like a record. It started with how many man-hours went into the construction of this model. He found a large old leather pouch with a drawstring at the top. The pouch had some kind of design and foreign type writing around the middle. The pouch seemed to be soft to the touch and old looking. The draw cord looked like small gold strings woven together. It was very heavy to be so small. Fearful of what might greet him in the pouch that had been stored there for a long time, he shook the contents out on the seat next to him, and then turned on the flashlight for a closer look.

It was an old ornament that looked like it could go on the hood of a car. A string was attached with a tag at the other end. On the tag was a note from Roger's father. It said the ornament had been picked up on one of his new engine endurance test flights to Greece. Even though the B-25 was a medium range airplane, it could fly twenty hours with only one crewmember, extra fuel tanks and wing drop tanks. Apparently, Roger's father was a test pilot and retrieved this ornament of Pegasus, a Greek mythical horse, on one of his trips.

The cockpit was now full of sunlight. I need to hurry and get home. Mother will want to know why it took so long to throw papers this morning.

"Leaving the house early will give me a chance to stop by the Library and get a book on ancient Greek mythology," he thought.

He found that Pegasus was a white flying horse that sprang from the body of someone called Medusa. The horse had wings and was the only one in the world. The horse in the ornament stood on its back legs pawing the air, its wings were spread apart as though in flight.

The note said the horse came from a Greek antiquities shop in the old part of Athens, Greece. The elderly proprietor, who walked with a long brass pole to steady his pace, said the marble and gold carving had been in his family for over a thousand years. The note continued to report the statue was found in the unearthing of some ancient ruins near the Acropolis many hundreds of years ago. The shop proprietor was alone without heirs to receive the statue at his passing; he became close friends with Roger's Dad and wanted to give Pegasus to him to protect him in his travels. The old man believed the statue contained mythical, magical powers of flight.

It should be placed in a special hole on top of the pilot's yoke. The ornament, according to the note, should be set in place by a person who had a true and kind heart, one who believed in magic with an open mind, a believer in ancient magical powers, and one who believed in day dreams. Only under these four conditions will the magical powers of Pegasus work.

"Yeah, tell me another one," Jay thought to himself, as he pondered what the book said. "But it would be fun to pretend that it was magic and could make the little bomber actually fly."

Jay couldn't wait for nightfall. He wanted this day to pass quickly so he could get back to the bomber. The first thing I'll try is going to be the horse thing — to test the magical powers of Pegasus.

The night passed quickly, and Jay hurried to finish throwing his papers. He rushed back to Roger's house and the bomber. Once inside, Jay made his way forward to the flight deck. When seated he opened the pouch with the little horse. As before he dumped it out into the co-pilot's seat. With his flashlight still on, he held it up and turned it around for a complete investigation. It seemed innocent enough, just a marble, jade and silver ornament. Jay leaned forward and, once again with his light, investigated the ornament's holder. It also looked okay so he placed the horse into the slot. It would not go all the way. The slot was full of dirt under the edges. Using his pocketknife he cleaned the dirt out. Again, he ever so slowly placed the horse into the slot and with a little pressure he wiggled it into its proper place. It seemed to lock into place with a snap. At the same time, small lightning streaks went from the horse to his hand and up his arm. Also, a strong wind seemed to go through the airplane whirling leaves and small branches around like a devil whirl wind.

When it stopped, the inside of the airplane changed into a real life-size bomber. Everything changed, even Jay. He turned around and flipped the starter switch for number one engine. Using military terms, he turned the switch for the starboard (or left) engine. The propeller started turning very slowly at first, and then the RPMs got faster and faster. The engine backfired a couple of times, and flames came out of the exhaust. Then it caught and started to run. He did the same with the number two engine, the port engine. Jay reached down and released the brakes. The ship began to move forward out of its parking area. The back yard disappeared, and a long runway stretched out in front of him. He turned for a practice run, and then stopped. He turned the ship around and went back to its parking place. He shut both engines off. As he removed the horse, the plane changed back to its original form. Jay placed Pegasus back in the pouch.

"I have to get permission from Roger before I can do this," he thought.

Jay leaned back in the seat thinking about what just happened. "Nobody will believe this. I'm not sure I do," he thought. Jay closed his eyes and went back over everything. The excitement and surprises that he encountered this morning made him very tired. Jay fell asleep.

Chapter 12
ROGER'S REASON

As the sun came up over the nose of the bomber, he could hear big guns off in the distance. Suddenly, he woke up and could hear his heart pounding so loud he thought it would wake the neighborhood.

He gathered his things, including the pouch with Pegasus, and hurried home. Today his mother planned to take the children shopping for school clothes. He needed to talk to Roger and make a deal to play in the airplane. He could see that the grass needed to be cut around the plane and the inside needed to be cleaned out. Maybe Roger would like someone to play with and help with some of the chores.

As he was leaving he ducked under the heavy row of bushes separating Roger's back yard…no…this secret airfield and the alley. He should cut some of these small limbs. No matter how carefully he tried to pass the bushes, he always got hit in the face with a limb or two. He stopped again for a long look at this wonderful thing and knew he couldn't wait another day to talk to Roger. He must have time in this brown bomber so he could fly important missions.

He had to think of some kind of a trade off. Roger didn't have any friends that he knew about. He didn't like to play outdoor games—any kind of games. This would be tough. Anytime they had a contest at school like baseball, football, spelling bee, Roger was the last one chosen. He wasn't dumb or anything, he just didn't know how to get along with other kids.

"This is our first home in a city," Roger's mother told Jay's mom. "We were always on the move. He attended five schools in as many cities in one year. Every time he made new friends, he had to leave them. His father was a major in the Army Air Corps researching and developing new types of aircraft, and the planes had to be tested in all kinds of weather conditions," she said remembering with concern.

"We moved all over the world and lived on Army air bases. Roger's father worked on secret projects, so we couldn't live in the same area as other service families. We were restricted from talking with other people on the base," she continued. "I'm afraid Roger does not know how to get along with children his age. Because your boy and girl have befriended him, he seems to be coming out of his shell a bit."

"At the end of the school day, Roger comes home and stays inside until time to go to school again," his mother confided. " He spends his time reading at home or at the Library, and he loves to work with his erector and chemistry sets," she concluded.

"Boy, I don't know how you do it, Roger." Jay said. "Just reading what I have to do for school is all I can handle," Jay admitted one day when they were talking.

But now Jay knew he must make friends with Roger and make a deal on the bomber. He must get started flying missions as soon as he could. No, the bomber needed to be cleaned inside and out first. The tall grass had to be cut and the bomber must be painted.

"Boy, if Mom heard me say I wanted to cut grass without being told, she would think I'm sick," he chuckled, as he hurried home.

Chapter 13
MONKEY WRENCHES

Jay's only thought the next morning was getting over to Roger's to see that brown bomber again. School started Monday and he needed to spend today making a deal with Roger and cleaning inside and around the bomber. He could use the hand sickle to cut the grass under her, but cleaning that plane was not his biggest problem.

His thoughts were so tied up with the bomber that he forgot about the first problem, big bad Billy. Billy was still mad about what happened at the Library, and he wanted revenge in the worst way. Jay made him the laughing stock of the neighborhood.

It's understandable why he would be so mad. Two weeks ago Billy and his stooges had all the money and bullied respect from frightened kids he needed. Today children no longer walked in groups when he came around. Much of the time, his three goons were not with him and he walked by himself. All of them feared they were being watched.

Jay watched for Billy. He knew that if Billy's goons were not with him the next time they met, he might resort to jumping Jay from behind bushes and settling the score. Jay thought that Billy believed he needed to pound Jay into the ground, so he could get the respect back that Billy thought he once had.

"Poor Billy," Jay confessed. "You have to feel sorry for him; he's always alone. Even the teachers know about what happened between Roger and Billy. Now they will always be on to him about things they once overlooked," Jay smiled sheepishly when talking with his sister.

If Jay wasn't careful, the Billy problem could slow him down with the work he needed to do on the bomber.

Chapter 14
THE SECOND MONKEY WRENCH

The first day of school started out badly. The next several weeks were no better. Jay spent too much time day dreaming about that wonderful brown bomber and talking to Roger about playing in his yard.

Because of that brown bomber, Jay had his second setback. Ever since the bell rang, Jay's mind had been on nothing but that airplane and convincing Roger to let him play around it. Jay didn't understand why Roger should mind. He would be there early in the mornings and on weekends. He stared out the window watching the birds in flight. Immediately his thoughts went to the brown bomber and how those birds could be enemy fighters coming after him. He should head for the cover of clouds. One of the fighters got behind him—he could feel the bullets hit his right shoulder—it really did hurt.

Then, he heard his name being called. He cleared his mind of the air combat thoughts and realized that the teacher, Miss Clements, had hit him repeatedly on the shoulder with her ruler. The rest of the class began to laugh.

"Jay," she scolded, "you need to do your dreaming at night in your own room. This is my room and my class, and I want your undivided attention to what I'm saying. Are we together on this?" she demanded.

"Yes, Miss Clements," Jay managed to respond, "we are together and I apologize." Jay thought that would end the matter, but Miss Clements had other plans.

Jay had to stay after school because of the little encounter with enemy fighters. He thought he would never get to talk to Roger. He had to erase both ten-feet long black boards before she told him the rest of his punishment.

"You are to write one hundred times, 'I will not daydream in my classes," Miss Clements said emphatically.

"Boy, this won't take long," Jay thought, "I can still catch Roger before he leaves the school ground."

As he started to write, Miss Clements caught him by the hand.

"You write that sentence here," she said, pointing to the middle of the board. You write it in large letters, so I can read it from the back of the classroom," she continued. "When you finish one line, you erase it and rewrite that sentence over again in the same spot. You will do this one hundred times for two days," she exclaimed. "Your day dreaming is not only keeping you after school; it's keeping me also," she complained.

Jay wrote as fast as he could, but it still took a long time. Miss Clements stopped him in the middle of the first line.

"Mr. Young," she scolded again. "Your handwriting needs some improvement. Either it improves quickly, or there'll be handwriting classes after school next."

"Could Miss Clements be a German secret agent?" Jay wondered.

He had to write slower so his handwriting would look better. It took him an hour and a half to finish his punishment. By the time he finished, Roger had left the Library and had gone home. Jay knew he must go home too if he wanted to stay on his mother's good side. His sister, Jan, would tell Mom about his problem, and he felt sure her story would be much better than his. Maybe if he walked faster, he would have time to go by Roger's house.

As he reached Roger's house, he convinced himself that he should stop. Roger's mother seemed glad to see Jay and invited him to come in. She directed him to Roger's room where he could talk with Roger.

"Roger," Jay asked excitedly, "why is there an airplane in your back yard? You have been over to my house many times to play with me and talk with Jan and even get me in trouble, but you never mentioned anything about an airplane." Jay continued, "Do you remember that time you and Jan were playing baseball in our side yard? You threw the ball to her, and she hit it hard—so hard that it went through the basement window. You and Jan started running to where I was, and I started running to where you were. As Jan passed me, she handed me the bat. There I was," Jay exclaimed, "standing there looking at the broken window with a bat in my hand when Daddy came out the side door. Well, you got me in a lot of trouble. After the spanking, I had to use all my money to replace that window. Do you remember that?" Jay questioned. "During all that time, you never said anything about that brown bomber in your back yard."

Roger said nothing; just sat on his side of his bed looking at the floor.

"Roger, why don't you answer Jay?" his mother said from the bedroom door. He got up and left the room leaving his mother and Jay looking at each other.

"I'd better be getting on home," Jay remarked quietly.

"Will you stay for dinner, Jay?" Roger's mother asked.

I'd like to but I'd better be getting home," Jay replied, "Mother doesn't know where I am."

"If I call your mother and ask her, would you stay?" she requested. "I would like for you to," she said in a very soft voice.

"Yes, if it's okay with Mom," Jay replied.

She called Jay's mother and got permission for him to stay for dinner. But his mother reminded him that tonight an air raid drill was planned, and Jay must hurry home after eating. Air raid drills occurred once a week, and they were usually without warning. But Jay's Mom often learned in advance about the drills. There were reports that the Germans developed a new rocket bomb that could reach the coastal cities of the U.S. If that were true, the air raid drills became more urgent to protect our cities. She also reminded him that he must get up early to throw papers.

"If Roger would let me in that bomber," Jay thought to himself, "I could bomb those rocket sites."

"Will you come in the kitchen with me while I prepare dinner?" Roger's mother asked, as she walked toward the kitchen. "Hope you don't mind not having meat," she added. "The market was out of meat this week."

"Anything is fine, Mrs. Wendel," Jay replied.

"Pull out a chair and sit down," she said, as Jay followed her into the kitchen.

Mrs. Wendel began to talk to Jay about her son.

"Roger told me about what happened with that bully, after I questioned him about it. He didn't want to. Miss Whitford called the day it happened to tell me about what took place and to check on Roger. She's a close friend of mine, and she told me something bad happened and she was worried about Roger. She called to see if Roger was all right and not hurt." She paused for a minute while she went to the pantry for some jars of home made vegetables. "Roger is very helpful to me," she said. "He helped me can all these items," she bragged, as she pointed to the pantry with many shelves full of canned foods. "Since his father died, Roger thinks he has to stay with me all the time."

"Did Roger's father die in the war?" Jay asked.

"No," she replied, "he died in a plane crash. He worked as an aeronautical design engineer and test pilot for the Army Air Corps. He helped to design and build the B-25. On his tenth test flight, after changing to more powerful engines, one caught fire and before he could escape, the engine blew up taking the wing off. Roger's father didn't have a chance to survive. That model in the back yard is like the airplane he flew." She paused to work with dinner for a moment.

"That plane in the yard was built to scale and used in the wind tunnel for testing. Just before the crash, they built a new model with added modifications for testing the new wing design required to accommodate new engines. The Air Corps did not need the first model so Roger's father talked them into selling it to him. They dismantled and shipped it here along with a mechanic to reassemble the airplane. It arrived the day of the funeral. It took about two weeks to put it together. It's an authentic replica of the Boeing B-25, medium range, twin-engine bomber. Only the size is different and the aluminum skin is much thinner than on the real airplane." Mrs. Wendel seemed well informed about the B-25 as she spoke to Jay. "Roger knew his Dad bought the airplane and that it would soon be delivered. They made plans to assemble and paint it as a team. After finishing they were going to hold a real christening and name the plane. His dad didn't tell anyone what the name would be. He planned to paint it on the nose after Roger went to bed the night before the christening."

"The day before the crash," Mrs. Wendel continued with the story, "Roger's father was called back to duty. They wanted to test the bomber with the new engines right away. Roger was asleep when the call came, and his dad didn't want to wake him. According to his orders, he should have returned the next afternoon to finish making plans for the plane."

"We got the news late the next afternoon," she said, as she set the plates and silver on the table. "What upset Roger so badly is that he didn't get to say goodbye to his dad before he died. He has not been inside that plane. I've tried to get him to play out there, but to no avail. Three weeks after the death of his father, Butch, his boxer, died. The dog was 10 years old. Roger decided the B-25 is a symbol of death. It killed his father, and somehow it's responsible for the death of his dog. He believes that everything that comes close to the airplane will die. So, he pulled inside himself and doesn't want to have anything to do with anyone. He won't leave me for a moment unless I insist. You and your sister are his only friends," she conceded, as she sat down across the table from Jay wiping the tears from her eyes.

"Do you want to play in the bomber, Jay?" she asked, as she noticed Jay becoming emotional also. "I saw you early in the morning looking over the bomber," she said. Jay started to apologize but she stopped him.

"You can play out there anytime and as long as you want," she insisted, as Jay squirmed nervously, "It doesn't bother me, and maybe Roger might forget why he doesn't like the airplane."

"Mrs. Wendel," Jay worried, "thank you, but maybe I should talk to Roger about this also. There's a note of some kind to Roger from his father. I didn't read it; it looked personal."

"Thank you for that, Jay," she responded. "Yes, I knew his Dad wrote a note to Roger. I don't know what it says. Every time he made a test flight, he wrote a note to Roger. I do hope you can help me get Roger out of his shell," she said, as she called Roger to come to the table for dinner.

Before leaving after dinner, Roger and Jay talked over the use of the airplane. Jay made Roger a deal he couldn't pass up.

"I'll give you two candy bars and a pack of gum every week in exchange for letting me play in the brown bomber," Jay offered, and Roger agreed.

Candy and gum were almost impossible to get because of the war. The major supplies went to the armed forces, and some ingredients were in short supply because of the source. Jay had an arrangement with a grocer on his paper route. He traded ten candy bars and five packs of gum each week for fifteen newspapers at a cost to Jay of thirty cents. The grocer could sell the papers for five cents each. Jay's cost was only two cents per paper, and the grocer's cost equaled the same amount. Roger wanted the candy and gum, and Jay wanted to use the bomber. They had a deal.

Roger thought he got the better part of the deal, and Jay didn't disagree with him because he still had eight candy bars and four packs of gum to sell, plus the use of the bomber. He felt like cream in a bottle of milk—he came out on top.

Jay had to hurry home so he could hear his radio programs. Two hours of heroes on secret missions—always helping to fight for

America against injustice in the world: Jack Armstrong, the All American Boy; Terry and the Pirates; Captain Midnight; and Sergeant Preston of the Yukon.

Later Jay wrote a letter to his Dad telling him about school, the brown bomber, and about the paper route. His mother put it in with her letter. The family finished dinner and Jay went to work cleaning the table and helping with the dishes. He asked to be first to take a bath and offered to bathe his little brother. His mother wanted to know what was wrong.

Everybody pitched in and helped because the air raid drill would sound in only thirty minutes. During an air raid drill, all outside lights must be off and heavy dark drapes drawn across the windows so no light will show. Every area has an Air Raid Warden that patrol's several blocks to make sure the homes and streets are dark. If you break the rule in any way, you will receive a citation and fine.

"Did you do something wrong at school or break something in the house?" Mother asked, wondering why Jay seemed to be so helpful.

"No," Jay replied, "I just feel good and want to show you that I'm the man of the house."

"Good, I just hope it'll last," she said, as she picked up her sewing and went into the parlor.

"I'm going to tell Mom that you had to stay after school because you were bad," Jan whispered.

"You do and I'll see that Roger doesn't come over anymore. We have a deal now," Jay retorted. "We are going to be good friends."

Jay went to bed early because he wanted to get up early for his first bomber mission. He set the alarm to go off at 4:30 A.M. He hoped the clock would not wake up his mother. She would ask why he left so early. He would tell her that he needed to finish so he could go to the Library before school. This was true—he needed to spend some time in the map section.

Chapter 15
MONKEY WRENCH THREE

When the alarm clock went off, Jay thought it was an air raid. All night he dreamed about flying and air raids on his secret airfield. Presently, his head cleared, he dressed quickly and went up to the attic to look for the old flier's cap and white scarf Dad gave him last year. The cap, scarf, and real flier's goggles went into the newspaper bag. He put on his leather jacket against the chill in the early September morning. Besides, Jay knew a pilot couldn't fly without his leather jacket.

When he got to the paper drop off station, the papers had not arrived. Something moved in the dark shadows—oh no, it was Billy, and he looked unhappy.

"What are you doing here, Billy?" Jay asked in surprise. He got that mean look on his face and started towards Jay.

"I'm here to even the score, dreamer," he winced.

"Why do we always have to fight?" Jay asked wondering why Billy was out by himself.

"Because I don't like you, wimp." Billy blurted out.

"You and my sister have something in common then," Jay replied, "she doesn't like me either, but we don't fight."

"Does she let you play with her dolls?" he sneered. "Maybe she'll let you wear one of her dresses after today," he said, as he started toward Jay. "I'm going to give you two raccoon eyes."

"Billy it's not like you to be here without your little army," Jay interjected. "You know, those stupid goons that follow you around and do all your dirty work." Jay said in the best John Wayne tone he could muster.

Jay backed away from Billy and fell over something—one of his goons on all fours directly behind Jay. The other two were on top before Jay could recover from the fall. They held Jay down while Billy sat on his stomach pounding Jay in the face.

"I'll work on that mouth of yours," he sneered, "and then I'll give you the two raccoon eyes. When I finish, you won't be able to eat or talk," he continued, pounding and muttering at the same time. "No teeth, a big fat bloody lip and you'll look like you're wearing sun glasses all the time." He hit Jay several times and suddenly stopped. The other three let go and ran off. Billy struggled to stand up, and then he ran off too.

Jay felt someone holding to his arms trying to lift him to his feet. It was Willy Harrison, the paper truck driver.

"Son, you have blood and cuts all over your face," he spoke with concern, "What happened here? Were they trying to rob you?" he asked. "I'll go down the street to the police box."

"No, please don't do that," Jay said, crying with the pain. "Please, just help me pick up my ring and customer cards," he managed to say between sobs.

"First, I'll clean up that face and patch it up," Mr. Harrison suggested. "We don't want the other boys to see you like this, do we?" he consoled Jay. "You know, boys don't cry—I have a company first aid kit in the truck," he said, as he led Jay back to his truck.

The other boys began to arrive while Mr. Harrison was cleaning Jay's face. He explained Jay had been attacked and asked the boys to get the papers from the truck.

"Look, guys, this is going to take some time," he suggested in a kind but firm voice. "Why don't you boys roll his papers for him so he can finish on time." They helped Jay like good team buddies.

"You have only one big cut and the rest are small," he reported. "Most of the blood came from your nose, but you need to go home and rest for awhile," he continued, "I'll get your area manager to throw your route."

"How big are the cuts?" Jay asked.

"It really looks like you slid on the side walk on your face." He smiled at Jay and added, "Either you have a hard head or he has soft fists, and you're going to have one big headache in about an hour."

"You may not want to report this to the police, but I do," Mr. Harrison explained. "We can't have robbers doing this sort of thing to the paper employees. Maybe they'll watch this place closely for the next few days. And more than likely, they'll want to talk to you about what happened," he added, as he opened the door of the truck for Jay to sit down.

They drove down the street to the police box and called for help. A newspaperman came to drive Jay home.

Chapter 16
THE HEALING

As Jay waited for someone to come to take him home, he began to realize that Mr. Harrison was right about the headache. And his right eye felt like it was swelling closed — it was getting hard to see.

Finally, someone came from the newspaper to take him home so Mr. Harrison could go on dropping his papers. When Jay got home, the police were there talking to his mother. As he climbed out of the car with the newspaper man, his mother saw him and started running toward him with her hands in the air. Jay had to bend down to hug her — she stood only four feet ten inches tall.

"Land o-Goshen," she used her favorite saying, "what happened to you?" she managed to ask, while she cried and talked at the same time. "How could something like this happen?" she exclaimed, as she turned to the policeman and demanded, "Where were you when he was attacked?"

"Is it all right if we talk with him about what happened?" the policeman asked Jay's mother.

"Yes," she replied, "but you'll have to do it inside while I work on his face. I want you two to see what it looks like."

Jay's mother checked him over and told the newspaperman and the police what she found.

"There is a small cut on his ear, an inch long cut above his eyebrow, several small scrapes on his chin and below his eyes," she recited his injuries, "and his lip is cut where his tooth came through," she added.

"Next time I won't try to talk, and I'll keep my mouth shut," Jay said, trying to be brave about the painful injuries.

"There won't be a next time," his mother scolded.

"We think he needs to go to the hospital and have a doctor check him out," the police officer insisted. The newspaperman agreed. Jay's mother asked the neighbor to care for Jan and Johnny. They weren't going to school today.

Jay and his mother were taken to the hospital in a police car. Jay had never ridden in a police car before.

"It's too bad Big Billy isn't in this car headed for the police station," Jay thought. "No, I'll take care of him myself."

When they arrived at the hospital, the doctor told Jay's mother that the newspaper owner called. He agreed to pay all the hospital bills for Jay, relieving her mind of that burden.

"I don't know who attacked me," Jay lied to the police. "Telling them they were men will throw them off Billy's trail," Jay thought.

The police waited for the hospital to release Jay and drove them home. The doctors put two stitches above Jay's eye, bandages on his ear and chin, and a patch over the swollen eye. When he looked in the mirror, he saw what Billy meant by raccoon eyes. Both of them were black.

His lips were so swollen he couldn't eat—that meant a lot of milk shakes. That would be great if they could get real milk. Rationing caused them to have to drink concentrated milk that tasted nasty unless you put chocolate or vanilla flavoring in the milk. They said his cut lip would take about eight to ten days to heal.

The next morning the newspaper printed a story and a picture of Jay explaining what had happened to him. His friends at school knew who beat him because one of Billy's friends bragged about how they got even with Jay.

Jay didn't worry about Billy this time. Only two things worried him—keeping his paper route and playing in the brown bomber. He couldn't wait.

That afternoon Billy stopped Jay in the hallway and asked him to come to his house. Billy's mother wanted to talk with Jay. "Jay, wait

I need to see you," Billy said, as he stopped Jay.

"What do you want," Jay said, with a disgusted gesture to Billy.

"My mother wants to talk with you," Billy said nervously, "Please, can you come to my house right now?"

"Where are your three friends?" Jay wanted to know.

"I don't know, they aren't my friends any more," Billy managed to get out.

"Who is going to be there?" Jay wanted to know.

"Just Mother, me, and you." Billy said.

"I guess so, Billy," Jay replied.

Chapter 17
THE BULLY'S DEN

Billy's Mother sat on the front porch when Billy and Jay arrived that afternoon. As they turned into Billy's yard, his mother met Jay at the top step. She looked at his face and tears ran down her cheeks. Putting her hands on Jay's shoulders, she pulled him close to her.

"I'm sorry," she said hugging him and crying. "I'm so very sorry, Jay. That's your name isn't it?" she continued asking questions. "Are the police going to take my baby to jail?"

"Baby," Jay thought, "that's the biggest baby I've ever seen." Out loud he said, "I don't know; if his three gooo....friends keep talking about what happened, he could go to jail."

Jay didn't know what Billy's mother said or did to him, but he was a changed person. No one ever knew what happened that early morning — the secret stayed with Billy, his mother and Jay.

To Jay's surprise, Billy was not as stupid as he let on. His grades improved, and he stopped bothering Roger and everyone else. The three goons didn't know what to make of Billy's new ways. They soon disappeared as a gang and began to fit in with the other kids in school. But because of their reputation, most of the kids were still afraid of Billy and his three ex-goons. It really did leave Billy isolated.

After almost two weeks, Jay was well enough to crawl inside the bomber. What else could happen to interfere with his playing in the bomber and going on secret missions?

Jay and Billy went to visit Roger to try to mend the bad feelings between them. Both Roger and Jay worked at forgiving Billy for his past behavior. When Billy saw the airplane, he seemed to change into a different person. The boys spent an hour cleaning the outside of the bomber. Jay found some paint in Roger's basement that could be used to touch up some of the bad places. When Roger saw the paint, he became very agitated.

"Painting the plane was something my Dad and I planned to do together," he bristled. Jay handed him the paint can and stepped back motioning him to go ahead and paint. Soon Billy helped Roger with the painting. They painted the bottom of the fuselage and the bottom of the wings a light sky blue for camouflage. Roger let Billy paint the numbers and other trim on the plane.

Roger's mother brought them some cold lemonade. She motioned from the back porch for Jay to come get the drinks.

"This is the first time Roger has been that close to the plane or paid any attention to it," she said, as she handed Jay the glasses. "Maybe this would be a good time to tell Roger about that package you found," she added.

Jay took the lemonade to the boys and they sat down under the wing. They drank the lemonade in silence. Finally, Jay approached the subject of the package.

"There's a package inside the plane under the left pilot's seat from your Dad, Roger," Jay said, as he motioned toward the cockpit.

Roger jumped up and ran for the bomb bay doors—the only way inside. He started to climb inside, stopped and sat down under the doors. He motioned for Jay to come closer.

"Jay, will you get the package for me?" he asked.

"Roger, you know I haven't healed up enough to crawl inside the plane. If I could, I would be inside right now working on something," Jay lied, hoping to get Roger to go inside for the package himself.

Roger sat there on the ground for a minute or so and then stood up inside the bomb bay and disappeared inside. Jay crawled to the bomb bay doors to look inside. Roger sat quietly in the left pilot's seat going through the package. He found the note from his Dad. He unfolded the paper and read it—a private message from a father to his son left to read in case the father didn't return. Roger's father knew that each time he left could be the last he would see his son. Roger leaned forward resting his head on the yoke and wheel sobbing softly. Jay climbed back out leaving Roger to grieve alone. As Jay's mother would say, "He has a right to express his feelings."

This had been a big day for Roger. He worked around the airplane and managed the courage to go inside and read the letter from his dad. Jay thought that he should go—when Roger came out of the plane, he might be embarrassed. Jay wondered why Billy disappeared.

He headed for the bushes at the end of Roger's yard to the shortcut that caused him to find the B-25 bomber. When he reached the path through the bushes, someone stepped out blocking the way. A few more steps and he realized it was Billy.

"On no, now what?" he wondered to himself.

"Don't leave me here alone with Roger," Billy said, waving both arms back and forth. "I don't know what to say or do," he said with concern.

"I think we should go home and leave Roger alone with his thoughts tonight," Jay replied also with concern for Roger.

"This really does look like a real airplane," Billy exclaimed. "Can it fly?"

"No," Jay replied. "It's a model Roger's dad bought to be assembled here," Jay said, feeling shrewd and clever, "It's like the real thing, but smaller."

Chapter 18
BILLY THE ARTIST

"Jay, Mother wants you to come over to our house," Billy said, as they walked along. "She sent me after you; she wants to talk to you, and I want to show you something."

When they reached Billy's house, his mother was sitting on the front porch and motioned for them to come near.

"Billy," she said, "there's a pitcher of iced lemonade in the refrigerator. Pour three glasses and bring it out. Bring the cookies in the jar also," she called after him. "You boys look hot and hungry."

"Yes ma'am, we are," Jay agreed.

"Billy told me that you and Roger are friends," she pondered. "That's good," she continued on. "Both Billy and Roger have lost their fathers to untimely death." She paused and then said, "Maybe they will find something in common."

While Billy and Jay drank their lemonade and ate the cookies, his mother went into the house. She reappeared in a few minutes with an old satchel. As she opened it, Jay could see it was full of papers. She pulled out a pad of drawings. They were of Billy's parents.

"This is what Billy likes to do," she said proudly. "But his so called friends made fun of his artistic ability, and he is ashamed of being talented," she said. "So, Billy is a bully at school and an artist at home."

Astonished at the work Billy could do, Jay praised him for his talent. As he looked over Billy's drawings, an idea hit him on how to use Billy's art ability with the bomber. He can paint a picture of

Pegasus on the nose of the plane and a bomb under the cockpit for each mission.

"Billy, do you think you could paint a large white horse standing on it's back legs pawing the air with it's front feet and with large wings spread out like it was going to fly?" Jay asked. "Also bombs for every bomb raid we go on and airplanes for the ones we shoot down?"

"Hey, that's a great idea," Billy agreed after Jay talked to him. "I can be a part of your plans," he said, looking very pleased.

"Goodnight, Mrs. Cromwell." Jay said, as he prepared to leave. He must get to Roger's so he could have things ready for his first secret mission tomorrow morning.

Chapter 19
THE REAL THING

When the alarm clock went off, Jay jumped out of bed and dressed as fast as he could without making noise. He tiptoed down the hall to the attic door. The blasted hinges squeaked as the door opened. His mother asked him many times to oil those hinges and he failed to obey her.

He ran up the steps two at a time and found his junk box as his mother called it. He grabbed his flier's cap, scarf, and goggles, placed them in his bag, and put on his leather jacket. Throwing his newspaper bag over his shoulder, he went on his way, but at the foot of the attic steps his mother stood waiting.

"Son," she questioned, "what's wrong? What were you doing in the attic, and why are you leaving so early?"

An alert pilot must be a quick thinker and one who can react swiftly in any situation.

"Well," he tried to sound calm, "the others live closer to the paper drop off station, and they have bikes so they can get the best places to sit where the light is better to roll the papers." This is the truth. He always sat outside the shelter in the semi darkness.

"Mothers want their sons to tell the truth, and they can tell when we don't," he reasoned to himself. After his mother weighed his excuse in her balance, she decided to let him leave without any more questions.

Because he was so early, Jay was the first one at the paper drop off station. It seemed very quiet except for the bugs flying around the light in the shelter. Jay felt lonely rolling papers by himself.

He looked out into the darkness and couldn't see the far off streetlights and house lights. The space around him looked darker and lonelier because of the shelter lights, and the eerie feelings made the hair stand up on the back of his neck. Rolling the papers faster, he began to whistle a tune and read the headlines of the paper to get his mind off his fears. Finally, he finished and left before the others arrived.

Throwing the route backwards allowed him to finish at his secret airfield and it worked faster than the other way. He had almost two hours before the sun came up to destroy his mind-time. That's what he called the time he spent inside his own secret thoughts. He could shut out the world and do or be whatever he wanted as long as it didn't hurt others or destroy property. Adults call this meditation. When someone Jay's age does it, they call it daydreaming.

"I can close my eyes and use the back of my eyelids as a movie screen," Jay thought. "It's like a movie that I produce, direct and star in. If I don't like the way it's going, I can back it up and change anything I want to without asking anyone's permission. And the best part is that I'm always the hero."

As he entered the secret airfield, his paper bag turned into a pilot's flight bag. Pilots keep their maps, secret mission orders, preflight check list, and a flashlight in the bag.

Earlier tonight they fueled the bomber for this important top secret, very dangerous, pre-dawn mission. To this point only the mission commander knew where this morning's flight was bound. While Jay ran a pre-flight check on all the controls, the commander met him under a wing to wish him luck and pass the secret orders to him. Jay served as the only crewmember this trip. The rest stayed behind because of the added weight of extra fuel tanks needed for this long-range secret mission. In fact, this mission was so secret the rest of the crew did not know the aircraft left.

Jay's flight would take him over the North Pole to come in through the enemy's back door. All of the enemy aircraft spotters and radar units were pointing the other way, south. They hoped that if Jay should be spotted, he might be mistaken for one of their aircraft coming from the north.

The engines were changed to the new secret silent faster ones. These engines were like the ones on the German's buzz bombs that destroyed London. The buzz bomb, a large torpedo shaped cylinder filled with hundreds of pounds of high explosives, was mounted on top of the new type of engine—shaped like a cone without a propeller. They took off from a ramp several hundred feet long and flew faster than any fighter making them near impossible to shoot down. These flying bombs originated from the west coast of France and flew towards London. Having no controls, the bomb flew until the fuel tank was empty. Unlike the buzz bomb, the brown bomber's engines sounded like a soft whisper. Jay stood right next to them to hear any noise. The success of this mission depended on secrecy.

A good pilot always checked his own airplane. Jay walked around and under the aircraft checking all the controls again. He checked the flaps, ailerons, stabilizer, trim tabs and the rudder. He did this by moving each one up and down or sideways after he removed the safety chock blocks.

A safety chock block looks like a giant clothespin that is wedged over the thin edge of the control. It keeps the wind from moving the controls while the plane is on the ground. In a high wind the controls could be damaged if not blocked.

Jay kept his hand over the front part of his flashlight to allow little light to escape. The secrecy of this mission remained his priority.

After the outside preflight checks were finished, Jay made his way back under the fuselage and crawled up through the bomb bay doors. As he walked forward to the flight deck, everything looked a little fuzzy. He didn't have time to check the new equipment that was added to Pegasus for this special mission. The clock shows almost 0500 (5:00 A.M. regular people time) and he must be back no later than 0630, if he made it back—about ten minutes before the sun came up.

Once on the flight deck, Jay sat down in the pilot's seat and removed Pegasus from the pouch placing him in the yoke. As he started to check the items on the preflight checklist, he noticed everything in the Pegasus started changing. Everything around him started to get bigger, things became real. He reached into his flight bag and pulled out his aviator's cap, goggles, white scarf and an old set of earphones he used on his home made crystal radio set. He wore his flight jacket and was ready to go.

After moving the yoke back and forth, turning the wheel right and left, pushing the right rudder pedal and then the left, he completed the inside controls check. Now it was time to start the procedure for the engines. These new type of engines required a new list of instructions. The left engine should start first. Start the blower, set the throttles, and flip all the necessary switches. He flipped the number one switch and pressed the red start button.

He could feel the plane shake when the new silent high-speed starboard engine started. Starboard was the right side of the aircraft. Port was the left side. At first the engine made a soft whining sound, then a swooshing sound, and a flame came out the end of the engine. The entire procedure took only four or five seconds. The same procedure was repeated for the port engine.

The instrument panel lights came on, and all the gauges pointed to their proper places. All levers were in take off position. He double-checked the preflight and take off list. Throttles in the idle position, flaps set at twenty degrees, parking brakes on, and landing gear lock on. The yoke and wheel had proper movement. The wheels on these new airplanes are not completely round. They are more like half of a wheel with two buttons on the right top half and three on the left top half. The air corps sergeant said they call it a wheel because in the old days of flying a complete wheel was used on all airplanes and lighter-than-air helium balloons.

The buttons on the wheel had their uses. There were two for the right thumb. One was red and it operated the eight nose guns. The light blue button operated the four guns mounted outside and below the cockpit—two guns mounted on each side. The buttons for the left thumb were also color-coded. The yellow one released the wing fuel tanks. The fuel tanks were used up first, and when they were empty, they could be released to fall to earth. The red and white checked button operated the bomb bay doors. Press it once and the doors opened; press it a second time and bomb load would drop; press it a third time and doors closed. A third button was marked "D" for double destruction. When it was pressed, all of the shipboard guns fired at once: all twelve guns plus the top turret guns. When all guns were locked in the auto mode and fired, the Pegasus flew in a complete circle of outgoing gunfire.

One more button was on the top right of the wheel—intercom for talking to the crew or other aircraft and control towers. There would be no need for that button on tonight's mission. Except for the intercom button, all buttons had safety flip covers over them. The cover must be flipped up before the button could be depressed.

All controls checked out clear, and Jay was now ready to go. Any delays at this point, and the mission would be scrubbed. As he turned to look over his shoulder to check the back, the plane grew longer. When he checked the new engines and wings, they grew bigger.

CHAPER 20
IN FLIGHT

After a final look at the preflight list, Jay took the wheel in his left hand and released the parking brakes with his right. When he freed his right hand from the brakes, he slid it upwards to the throttles and slowly moved them forward for maximum thrust. At the same time his feet were on the rudder pedals moving them ever so lightly to guide the Pegasus straight down the runway.

Looking out the window into the darkness, Jay could see the bushes and trees rushing by so fast they were just a blur. He could not distinguish between the darkness and the bushes. Everything rushed by so fast; he began to worry if he could keep the plane out of the bushes and on the runway. Ahead several hundred yards a light marked the center of the airstrip. All he needed to do was head for it. At first that light seemed a long way off, but as it grew larger and brighter, the bouncing and shaking began to become smoother. He knew the end of the runway must be near.

"Oh no!" he thought, "Will the back yard be long enough for a clean take off with this over weight load? I wish I hadn't thought of that." The throttles were set at a full one hundred percent. It's too late to worry now. The bomber rolled very fast down the runway. Pressure from the high speed pushed him back into the seat. He pulled back on the yoke with all his strength and the nose started to lift. The nose wheel lifted off the ground. He had to guide Pegasus down the runway with the rudder while pulling back on the yoke at the same time. If in pulling back he put too much pressure on one foot or the other, he would veer off the runway. He could snap off one of the wings causing the plane to cartwheel and crash into one of the houses. The explosion could wipe out an entire block.

"I've got to get these negative thoughts out of my mind and concentrate on the job," Jay thought, as he worked at maintaining equal pressure on both rudders and backpressure on the yoke.

Suddenly, he could feel the tires freewheeling as the bomber lifted off the ground. The bouncing and shaking stopped and the sound of the landing gear retracting and the doors closing filled the cockpit. He was airborne and he could see the tops of the trees passing by the windows.

"Where did they go?" Jay whispered in amazement, "Where did all the back yards and houses go?" He wanted to look out the window but could not break free of the backpressure. All he could see was blackness and stars.

The whine of the engines grew faster and faster as the Pegasus began to answer to the controls much easier. He pulled back on the yoke very lightly and pushed the left rudder about five degrees at the same time slightly turning the wheel to the left.

The plane climbed very slowly in a turn. The backpressure began to go away. The left wing dipped down about twenty degrees and he could not see the town below. Instead he saw lights from several small towns. Everything looked far away and lonely.

He had been in the air for about three minutes when he noticed his altitude passed ten thousand feet. He will need to fly this course for another two minutes and level off at fifteen thousand feet. At fifteen thousand feet he changed to a compass reading of 045 degrees. He'll fly this reading for another four minutes. At the end of this climb, he should be at thirty thousand feet and using oxygen. The air is thinner and he can fly even faster.

The outside temperature dropped to 60 below zero. Inside the plane it stood at 45 degrees. Heat from the engines channeled inside to warm the cockpit. Jay felt comfortable in his heated flight suit. At ten minutes into the mission, he adjusted the throttles to one hundred percent. Again, he changed the heading to a course that would take him over Greenland. Once there, he changed the heading to 090 degrees. At that point he could set Pegasus on autopilot.

Chapter 21
CLOUD DANCING

Cloud dancing is a phrase used by pilots when flying between the moon and the clouds. The bright full moon casts a shadow on the surface below that can be seen as though it were daylight. Bombardiers referred to this condition as "a bombers moon." Jay thought, "Tonight is such a night."

From the air the brightness reflects off everything; rivers, lakes, buildings, railroad tracks, roadways, bridges and anything that moves. But tonight along the route there will be almost a complete cloud cover. When he reaches within an hour of the target, the sky will be completely clear. As for now, the clouds have a break now and then. Through the breaks the ocean can be seen below. Thirty minutes ago Jay passed over a large convoy of ships on its way to England with tons of war equipment and supplies. He felt sure there were enemy submarines lurking in the area. It's possible only half of those ships will reach their destination. Many will be sunk.

Pegasus, the bomber's name that Billy painted on the nose of the plane along with a large white horse with wings, flew east with the moon on the starboard (right) side of the aircraft. Jay thought about the name Pegasus. According to Greek mythology, Pegasus was a white flying horse with a long mane and tail and wings. Although all warplanes were given names by their crew, this name was special. Like the horse, the bomber is one of a kind.

As Pegasus flies over the clouds, a silhouette of the bomber is cast downward. The angle of the moonlight striking the plane caused three separate milky white circles around the bomber's reflection. The silhouette of the plane hurrying to its destination resembled the erratic flight of a butterfly. It darted from cloud to cloud, rising and falling, jumping to the right and then to the left as it followed the hills and valleys of the clouds. The shadow is the only company Jay and Pegasus will have on this special, dangerous mission. This flight will take Jay and the magic B-25 bomber deep into the enemy's homeland. Without cloud cover in this part of the North Atlantic, Jay might see some icebergs below. However, he's lucky that there is a complete overcast sky tonight. On a clear night, an enemy sub running on the surface to charge its batteries might spot him and radio his position to home base. Also, on a clear night, he would not have the company of the dancing silhouette.

Watching that other plane down below, Jay was left with an eerie feeling. The black shadow appeared small, and then it grew bigger as the cloud formation grew taller. Touching the top of the cloudbank, it wiggled along for a few hundred feet, and then disappeared into the vast darkness below. A few seconds later it appeared again, and the chase began anew. The clouds were all around Jay and Pegasus. They were tucked into the clouds like Grandma tucked him in a feather bed covered with quilts. The feeling always made him feel warm and safe. The soft white clouds looked inviting on the moon side and black and lonesome on the backside.

In spite of the solid cloud cover and the bouncing up and down, right and left, the automatic pilot kept the bomber on its preset course. This leg of the flight is the easiest part of the mission. Pegasus didn't fly around clouds but it darted right through them. As the clouds passed by the windows, they looked like puffs of smoke, and it seemed wet, dark, lonely and bumpy. The plane shook and rattled so badly, Jay thought the new engines might fall off.

From the outside of the clouds, they resembled big chunks of soft cotton. Sometimes they were caught in an updraft and jumped up suddenly a couple hundred feet, but the automatic pilot brought them back to proper altitude and correct heading. Once again in the clear, Pegasus settled down, and Jay could hear the soft hum of the engines. The sound of the engines along with the wind passing by the windows made him feel lonesome, like he was back on the paper route all alone.

Chapter 22
SECRET ORDERS

Jay must get his thoughts back inside the cockpit and on this almost impossible, very dangerous mission. In about three minutes the course must be changed. This entire secret mission covered "real time" of about ninety minutes, but in the magic bomber ten minutes of "real time" equaled two hours of magic bomber time. So the trip from base to target and back equaled eighteen hours of magic bomber time.

It's time to open the secret orders and set the new course. Jay took out the envelope the flight commander handed him before he boarded Pegasus. Inside the envelope he found an overlay map that he placed over the charts in his flight bag. It gave him the flight route pattern to the target city and the flight pattern of the bombing run. The homeward bound flight plan for the return trip would be different.

Schweinfurt, Germany, the target city for tonight, is known for its war factories, oil refineries, and a ball bearing factory. Other oil refineries in Germany, Romania, and Hungary were important, but only one ball bearing manufacturing plant existed in German occupied territory. Ball bearings were very essential to the enemy's war effort. All equipment that moved overland, in the water, or in the air used hundreds of ball bearings. Without these bearings and other essential material, such as oil, the war could soon be over. The Army Air Corps made several raids on this city. They damaged the oil refineries, but did not touch the ball bearing factory. Since all equipment used ball bearings, if this plant could be destroyed or crippled, it could indeed shorten the war. Jay thought, "Everything that rolls or turns on a shaft uses ball bearings."

On the overlay map were two red marks—Berlin and Nuremberg, Germany. Both were heavily armed with hundreds of anti-aircraft guns and searchlights. His fuel did not allow him to go around these cities. If he wanted to go home, he must fly directly over them. The instructions were to fly low—the new secret low noise, high-speed engines would be tested for the first time. His speed will help to hide him. By the time the aircraft spotters and gun crews hear him, he will have passed their observation zones. He hoped the new radar could not pick him up at the low altitude he will be flying.

He removed the navigational charts and maps from his flight bag and laid them on his lap. Reaching overhead he switched on the red nightlight. Looking down, he was shocked to see a newspaper instead of maps. The newspaper should have been delivered to the Smith house at 1241 7th Avenue before the mission. He guessed he would have time to do that after breakfast while on his way to school.

"Of course," Jay complained to himself, "the maps and charts were at the bottom of the flight bag."

Chapter 23
THE RAID

So far everything is according to plan. Of course, everything up to now has been easy. If he can get into the staging area without being spotted, drop the bombs and get back out again, that will be great.

"Gee," Jay said out loud, "things have gone so easy that I'm afraid something bad is going to happen. I'm three hundred yards ahead of the supply train without being detected."

Just outside of the factory doors Pegasus will change into a larger plane. That will give Jay full advantage of the entire plane and its capability. He will have full use of the guns — the firepower will be awesome.

The new course to Schweinfurt is south, southeast, flying at tree top level along the railroad tracks from Berlin and Hamburg until he reaches the city. He could see a large landmass ahead as the cloud cover disappeared. Inland the moon reflected on lakes and waterways. The rails running to Berlin and beyond reflected in the moonlight. He hoped the heavy anti-aircraft emplacements around Berlin would not spot him. After the raid they would be on the alert. Things will not be so easy.

When he reaches Schweinfurt, he will still be following the rail lines. The ball bearing factory is underground, but the staging area where all the workers gather for their change of shift is above ground in a very large building. Supplies and raw materials are left in the staging area for about two hours every morning. The new shift will move them down to the manufacturing rooms below. There is a large opening in the ground with an over sized elevator to move supplies, equipment, and people to storage areas below the ground. The manufacturing areas are next to the storage rooms. Jay's mission is to fly inside the building firing the ship's guns, drop the bombs down the elevator shaft, and leave the building before the explosions. He hoped firing the guns would keep the guards' heads down and allow the workers to flee.

During this early morning shift change is the only time the doors on both ends of the building remain open. When Jay spots the lights of the city, he will drop to tree top level, pass the city quickly, then lower his speed to stalling speed hoping he will not be spotted. The factory is fifteen miles southeast of the city. The rails will lead him directly there. The train carrying supplies and the day shift will be his landmark. He must arrive at the factory at the right time so all the doors will be open. Both ends of the complex must be open for the raid to be a success.

Jay flew far ahead of the train, and he hoped this could save many lives of the labor force. The moment he is spotted, the searchlights will go on, the gun crews will hurry to their posts, and the doors will be closed. When the doors close, the train will be safely outside. From the intelligence reports, the off going shift remains below ground until the on coming workers have unloaded the supply train. The guards will be exposed to the oncoming danger and, unfortunately, many of the underground workers as well.

The magic bomber neared the target and just seconds before entering the building, the alarm sounded, searchlights lit up the sky, and soldiers and guards ran inside. The doors remained open as they hoped to get the supply train safely inside the building. The enemy thought they were having an air raid from above. The minute they discover Pegasus is inside their building, the doors will start to close. Intelligence reported that it takes ten minutes for the large doors to completely close, thus giving Jay enough time to complete his mission and be safely out and on his way home.

Just before he entered the building a gun crew spotted him and started shooting. They got off a dozen or two rounds and then stopped. They were missing Pegasus and hitting the building. Once Pegasus entered the building the ground troops began shooting. Jay spotted soldiers running towards a large control panel next to the door. This must be the housing for the control switches for the doors. Using the buttons on the wheel, Jay started shooting all of the guns from Pegasus. The soldiers ran for cover as did all the others in the building. He spotted the elevator next to the railway loading platform. The elevator doors were open, but the elevator stayed down under ground. Great! It was a perfect opening for the bombs to drop into the under ground area without having to blast open the elevator doors. Jay opened the bomb bay doors, got ready to release the bombs and continued to keep the guns shooting. Things were still going fine.

Bomb release time is only three seconds away. Okay, ready…, one…, two…, three…, and release. Unaware of the next move, Jay was caught off guard. The weight of the bomb, two thousand pounds, was no longer a factor for the operation of Pegasus. Suddenly, the plane became lighter and jumped up thirty feet or more. The approach plan to the door would have to be changed.

Jay climbed too high and the doors were beginning to close. He pressed the normal button hoping the plane would go back to model size, but nothing happened. And the doors were closing fast. Jay thought more speed might help so he shoved the throttles to max. Pegasus lunged forward throwing him back into the seat. His forward view became somewhat obstructed because the seat moved back a little bit. By the time he adjusted his seat, his altitude showed too high and the doors were a very short distance away. But the shape of the magic plane changed back to normal and it looked like they might be safe. Jay's luck was holding up.

To exit through the almost closed doors, Jay must turn the wings at a forty-five degree angle to the left. He was still in trouble. Hanging down from the top of the doors were large lights. They hung on metal poles that extended downward about fifteen feet. Jay decreased the wing angle to ten degrees and pulled back on the yoke just a little. This caused the ship to dip somewhat before starting upward. The wings cleared the lights, but one hit the windshield on the left side where he sat. Glass covered everything. A piece hit Jay just above his right eye. He could not take his hands off the wheel to check. He gained more altitude to get away from the area before the bombs went off. Boy, did they go off. The bomb blast created a great shock wave that rocked the plane back and forth like a big ship on the ocean.

Jay needed to gain altitude to twenty five thousand feet and head south very quickly. He couldn't go back the same way he came or they would spot him. The plan called for him to fly at this altitude for thirty minutes, drop to tree top level and head west out over the Atlantic. Home base should be reached in five and a half hours. He had a lot of work to do while he was homeward bound.

Chapter 24
HOMEWARD BOUND

All of the extra fuel tanks were now empty and must be disconnected from each other and from the ship's fuel lines. Four tanks were in the bomb bay area, two in the waist gunner's area, and one back where the tail gunner sits. They were still using one of the extra tanks. After it's empty, they would finish the trip on the wing tanks.

The used tanks should be dropped out through the bomb bay doors. Large openings with screw-on caps were used to fill the tanks. These caps must now be removed so the Atlantic's water could fill them and they would sink out of sight. Moving the tanks seemed easy, but getting them through the bomb bay doors was a different story. With the doors open, a draft caused a downward suction. Jay should wear his parachute, but it caused him trouble moving around in the narrow walls of the bomb bay area. Of course, working around one still operating tank didn't help matters any. He removed the chute and could work much easier. By the time he moved the tank from the rear gunner's area, the ship started to cough as though choking for fuel. The last tank now showed an empty gauge. Jay hurried back to the flight deck to switch the fuel line back to the wing tanks. With the one remaining tank taking up space in the bomb bay, he could not move easily. As they say, it was no "Sunday walk in the park." He felt like he was walking a tight rope. Once he got back to the flight deck and flipped the switches, the engines snapped back and started running again. "This is the last time I'll try this type of mission alone," Jay thought.

Getting back to the now empty tank, Jay thought it would be easier to work on it from the rear. He felt there would be less danger for him by not having to work his way around the tank again. All the restraining straps were now loose, and the tank dangled by a small fuel line. When free of that line, the tank would drop into the Atlantic. He managed to free the tank and slide it to the doors ready to dump. As it started to move, Jay noticed the fueling caps were still in place. With the caps still on the tank would float. Jay would have to turn the plane around and shoot holes in the tank so it would sink. This would use fuel that he needed to get home. Somehow Jay had to stop the tank from falling and remove the caps. It was taller than Jay and weighed more too. As it slid by him he ducked under a bomb-supporting beam and placed his shoulder against the tank. It stopped sliding and Jay reached for a wrench. His shoulder moved a little and he went down on one knee. After stabilizing himself, he reached the wrench and removed the caps. Just about that time Pegasus hit an air pocket and dropped a couple hundred feet. The plane stopped its fall with a jolt causing the empty tank to fall free from the bomber, along with Jay.

"Help, help, help!" he shouted. He could see he was free of the ship. The tank knocked him up against one the bomb bay doors. He grabbed a support bar on the door with both hands. He could see the tank falling into the water with a big splash. He could have been with it, and still might be if he can't get back inside.

The wind tore at his flight suit and he froze with fear. At two hundred miles per hour the air felt very cold, and the wind was so strong he was losing his grip. His eyes burned and watered, and he couldn't keep them open in the howling wind. He tried to remember where his goggles were. Then it came to him, they were on his head over his cap. He couldn't move them in place with his hands because he couldn't let go of the plane and hang on with one hand against the powerful wind. Mustering all his strength, he very slowly and painfully pulled his body up to his hands and slipped the goggles into place.

"Here I am," he screamed, "hanging on five hundred feet above the Atlantic, with no parachute, my hands are freezing, and I don't know if I can hold on."

He tried to move closer to the center of the bomb bay opening. Hand over hand was out of the question. He must hold with both hands.

"Help, help, help," he yelled, "Now how stupid can I get," he thought, "There is no one around to hear me."

He managed to get to the middle of the bomb bay and swing one of his legs up over the center support bar of the bomb racks, but he couldn't pull himself up into the airplane with the power of the wind acting against him.

"If I can't make this work, I may fall into the Atlantic," he thought anxiously. "That will be really nice," he said out loud, "lost at sea and nobody would know it; they think I'm in school."

Pegasus hit another air pocket and dropped again. This time it threw Jay high enough that he ended up back inside the plane. He grabbed the support and pulled himself inside. He got to his feet and rushed back to the flight deck to close the doors. Falling into the pilot's seat, he rested for a few minutes. He thought about his fear of darkness and monsters in the night and knew he would never be afraid of that again.

Rechecking the autopilot setting on Pegasus, he noticed his head ached. He checked the cut for bleeding, but it seemed to be dry. As he settled down and relaxed, he dropped off to sleep. After a while, the plane started to climb to a higher altitude and a few bumps in the air woke him. When he looked out he could see the lights of several small towns. Just then the Pegasus engines changed pitch as they throttled back.

"Great, I must be home!" he thought. They banked to the left and started to drop faster. Now he could see the field ahead. Field, it looked like back yards. As they came closer and the altitude dropped lower, it changed to a long landing strip. Rolling along the strip after the touch down, the ship slowly changed back to its original size. Pegasus swung around and stopped at its tie down spot.

Jay put all his maps, scarf, hat, and goggles back in his paper bag and grabbed the paper that must go to the Smith's house at 1241 7th Avenue. He removed the Pegasus from the yoke. Holding it up in the light, he marveled at the events he just experienced. Placing it back in its pouch, he stored it in the drawer under the seat. He crawled back to the bomb bay doors, stopped, looked around, and shaking his head he crawled out of the airplane. Jay walked slowly around the bomber checking for any damage. Everything seemed to be okay. Throwing the canvas bags over his shoulders, he crossed the back yard (the field) and ducked under the hedge and into the alley. Going through the hedge, a branch struck him across the face sending a sharp pain through his head.

He must hurry home, clean up, eat breakfast, finish his morning chores, and go to school. He could deliver the Smith's paper on the way to school since they lived only a block from his house.

When he entered the kitchen, Jay dropped the paper bags near the back door and gave a sigh of relief.

"Not there Jay, you know better than that. Put them away in the cloak room on their special hook," his mother said, as she finished setting breakfast on the table. His little brother had a few words to say about his being late. Before Jay could answer, his mother stopped his response by telling Johnny to mind his own business. Johnny, at only five years old, liked to get Jay and Jan in trouble.

Jay's mother tuned the radio to her favorite news and weather station. The news commentator reported a story about a special one plane-bombing raid on a very important enemy war plant. The single plane and the brave pilot got away safely. With little loss of life, the plane completely destroyed the factory.

Jay sat listening in disbelief. He thought he might have dreamed the raid.

"It's about time our side showed some success," his mother said, reaching across the table to hand Jay his breakfast. "What happened to your face, Jay?" she asked.

"I guess I must have cut myself ducking under the hedge at Roger's house," Jay replied.

"Well, you must be more careful in the future, okay," she added.

Gathering up his schoolbooks and heading out the back door, Jay heard his mother yell after him.

"Wait for your sister," she said. Jay and Jan were in the same grade so they walked to school together. Of course, they always stopped by for Roger, and lately Billy joined them. They dropped off the newspaper Jay needed to deliver. As they continued on to school, Jay began to wonder.

"Did I get this wound ducking under Roger's hedge," he thought, rubbing the cut on his head, "or did I really fly out of that enemy building and catch that light with my windshield?" He looked up at a warplane flying over just then and thought, "I guess I'll never know."

What do you think?

THE END

Printed in the United States
87484LV00002B/36/A